Original Korean text by Jae-eun Jo
Illustrations by Jeong-seon Lee
Korean edition © Yeowon Media

This English edition published by big & SMALL in 2016
by arrangement with Yeowon Media
English text edited by Joy Cowley
English edition © big & SMALL 2016

Distributed in the United States and Canada by
Lerner Publishing Group, Inc.
241 First Avenue North
Minneapolis, MN 55401 U.S.A.
www.lernerbooks.com

ISBN: 978-1-925248-63-0

Printed in Korea

# Up and Down

Written by Jae-eun Jo
Illustrated by Jeong-seon Lee
Edited by Joy Cowley

big & SMALL

This is our house.

The basement is down at the bottom.
The living room is in the middle.
I sleep up at the top.

This is our garden.

The plants are up,
on top of the earth.
Their roots are down
deep in the earth.

9

Mom takes us to the park.

The trees grow up.
Their roots grow down.

This is the pond in the park.
We sail our paper boat
on top of the water.

Fish swim under the water.

Look at the new building.
The floors go up, up, up.

14

The foundations go down, deep into the ground.

15

Come and see our puppet show.
The puppets are up
on the stage.

We are down under the stage,
making the puppets work.

Our city has a subway.
The entrance is up on the road.

We get our tickets in the middle.
The train is down at the bottom.

Let's go to the mall.
There are stores at the top
and stores in the middle.

At the bottom is the parking lot.

Dad takes us to the ship.
The ship has upper decks
and lower decks.
On the upper decks
are the passengers.

On the lowest deck
are the sailors
who make the ship go.

Up and down! Up and down!
Stand outside and look around.
What goes high to the sky
and what is underground?

24

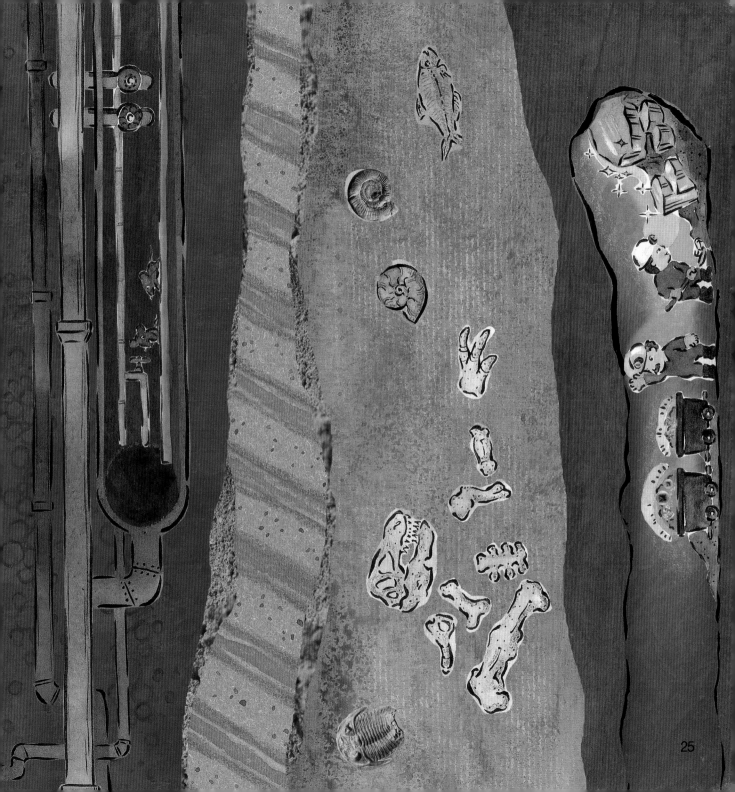

25